Parking Lot Adventures

Drawn & Written by
Omar MrOz

Introduction

After my first week working in the parking lot, the local security guard advised me to carry a pen and a small pad of paper to write license plate numbers on. I ended up drawing comics instead.

I didn't exactly attend college in order to become a parking lot attendant at a busy grocery store. I was extremely motivated and excited to get a degree in video production in order to make my way out to Hollywood and be the big time famous comedian/action hero/celebrity/director I've always envisioned my self becoming. I graduated with plenty of awards at the top of my class and landed a terrific position as a video contractor at a secluded local Philadelphia Cable station which in turn led me to creating and producing my very own comedy TV show called "The Mr.Oz Show." The Mr.Oz Show was rather well received by the 13 some odd people that actually tuned into to watch it every evening at 8:30 pm and the season finale even won two Telly awards in the comedy and entertainment category.

Convinced of the show's legitimate entertainment value, I quickly began shopping the show to major television networks. Amidst the arrival of multiple rejection letters from agents and TV networks I was sadly informed that a major cable corporation had purchased Philadelphia's best kept secret TV studio and will be terminating all video contractor positions immediately. Subsequently there was all this coverage about a recession on the national news. Then the Mr.Oz Show was quickly pulled off the local airwaves and the ample amount of job listings on the internet was reduced to digital dust. Finding a new TV job, let alone a TV network that was interested in the Mr.Oz show seemed to be turning into an unobtainable goal.

I began searching for jobs that were completely removed from my field of expertise. My neighbor mentioned that the local natural grocery market was a great company to work for and they also offered team member discounts. It sounded like a really solid idea considering bills were piling up and I was eating like a vagabond. I applied to the position at the store and spent several months trying to convince the managers to interview me. Finally one day they called me in to interview for a dishwashing position. I got a haircut, put on my best sweater, and went in for the interview. Several days later, I was informed that I didn't get the position. Consequently I fell into a minor pit of depression listening to lots of The Smiths and Morrissey and started growing my hair long. While trying to continue producing material for the now imaginary Mr.Oz Show I was also escaping into the strange private world of claymation. After 11 months of scraping around for freelance video jobs I returned to the grocery store continuing to inquire about any job opportunities. I even handed the assistant manager a piece of paper that I had written in large bubble letters: "fully functional human being equipped with arms and legs with full availability ready to work as soon as possible!" Surprisingly this worked because she laughed and told me I can come in to interview for the only current available position- the parking lot attendant position.

I arrived at the store for my 2nd job interview, and this time I purposely let my appearance go as an attempt to fit in with the look of general employee populace at the store. I hadn't shaved in over a week; my hair was a long disastrous mess and I was wearing my ripped up "Nightmare Before Christmas" hooded sweat shirt along with a pair of skeleton bone graphic gloves. After a few quick questions concerning my ability to endure the elements outdoors and organic food practices, they had finally granted me access to their work force!

The first time I stepped out onto the concrete I knew instantly that this was my new "stage" to perform on. As an actor, I instantly assumed the role of my newest character: the Parking Lot Guy. The Parking Lot Guy was quickly struck with a feverish case of narcissism, convincing himself that girls were always looking at him and checking him out. His duties at the job consisted of directing, managing, and monitoring traffic flow in a very confined parking lot with only 83 parking spaces. The only other available parking was next door inside a ground level garage that almost everyone refused to park in thanks to a dysfunctional ticket validation system and the misconception that it was underground. He was also in charge of reporting and towing any motor vehicles that surpassed the 2 hour parking limit.

My severe isolation from the store and other team members while working outdoors was quickly recognized. A friendship between the security guards and my self was formulated since we worked together in the timing and towing of motor vehicles and they frequently did their rounds outdoors too. During the conception phase of towing a vehicle the security guard advised me to keep a pen and small pad of a paper in my pocket in order to write down license plate numbers or any other sort of intelligence I gathered outside. I arrived to my job the next day with my pen and a small stack of printing paper in pocket that I trimmed down to 5" by 4" rectangle pieces. As the traffic from the lunch rush depleted, I summoned the pen and paper, then just like all those stale moments in school classrooms, I began doodling. The doodle transmuted itself into a brief crappy little comic strip. The next day was extremely slow in regards to traffic flow. I spent the majority of the afternoon watching a little bird peck away at bread crumbs that had been mysteriously donated to the concrete. Once again, I retrieved the pen and paper from my pocket and began drawing the silly little bird that hopped about my feet. Suddenly I became this resourceful rogue artist in the parking lot. There were numerous surfaces to draw upon; most frequently I exploited the small ledge spaces that the towering parking lot light poles provided at their base end which was directly at my chest level, the perfect height for me to draw while standing around. An innovative obsession with telling the microscopic adventures in the parking lot structured its way into my mind and I began avidly rereading my own strips to captivate my own attention both at home and in the parking lot!

Several months into the job and the traffic patterns became extremely routine and obvious. I tried to draw one parking lot adventure per work shift, this was only possible on acutely slow summer days, and much more difficult during the busy winter months. I usually ended up completing about 2 to 3 adventures a week, especially once I anteed up the level of drawing skill that is progressively visible as you turn every page in this comic book. I am personally very amused by the noticeable difference of drawing skill from the first several parking lot adventure pages compared to the final pages. The colder months also made it very difficult to draw outside, once the temperatures reached freezing levels, the ink in my ball point pen turned very stubborn, and barely made an impression on the paper. So I found a spot inside the next door garage in the stairwell that provided a remarkably solid drawing surface (on a step) and warmer temperatures that the pen could perform better in.

Avoiding my duties on the job and writing the comics were mostly a result of my fractured and crumbling faith in humanity, a problem that started spiraling out of control within a month of working in the lot. I observed an immense amount of poor judgment, reckless driving, bitter antagonized parents, disgruntled stakeholders, littering, disrespect, and most of all, forgotten shopping carts. The "not going to return my shopping cart" epidemic was extremely rampant at this particular store. Stakeholders would rarely return the shopping cart that they used to transport their groceries out to their motor vehicles. The cashier assistants were technically in charge of collecting the abandoned shopping carts from all corners of the lot, but these employees were generally too stoned, slow, or busy with indoor obligations. Somehow it gradually became my responsibility, because in the eyes of the stakeholders, that's what I was there for, a constant shepherd for the cross hatched metal baskets on wheels. Witnessing this constant lassitude and irresponsibility with out the ability to fully comprehend the reasoning behind it caused my faith in humanity to rapidly deteriorate. Countless situations with hostile stakeholders continued to drag my faith in humanity below surface level while a suspicious correlation between my parking lot job and the lack of interest from the female populace began creeping its way into my mind.

With so many pretty women frequenting the store, I couldn't resist taking an interest in some of the ones I'd see every day in the parking lot but the largest crush I developed was for this phenomenally beautiful personal trainer that worked at the sports club next door. I knew practically nothing about this girl except that she was surrounded by this alluring vitality, physically intoxicating, and she possessed a smile that could vaporize any affliction. I decided to take advantage of the upcoming Valentines Day holiday as a channel to reach out to her. The results of that particular romantic endeavor are chronicled throughout the final pages of these parking lot adventures.

These comics were all drawn on 5" by 4" cuts of paper while I was on the clock, outdoors amongst various weather elements in a parking lot with a crummy blue ball point pen. I draw entirely free-hand, straight from what I envision in my brain, no

pencil sketching, no mapping out of panels and se-
quences. Each panel was conceived, drawn, and
lettered in between small fractions of time directing
traffic. I want to share these parking lot adventures
with you the reader, and I am presenting them in
their natural raw state of existence. There is no
spelling or grammar check, no digitally enhanced
imagery, nothing you see in the comic strips has
been altered in any way. These are the life size
scanned pages that I nursed in my rear jeans
pocket during the course of a year working in a
busy parking lot. Please keep all of that in mind as
you read through this comic. Without any further
ado, I present to you my Parking Lot Adventures.
Enjoy!

-Omar MrOz

The Parking Lot Guy

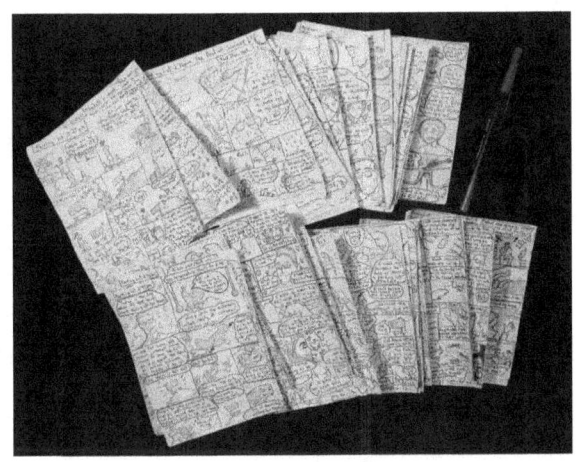

The Parking Lot Adventures

15

26

35

44

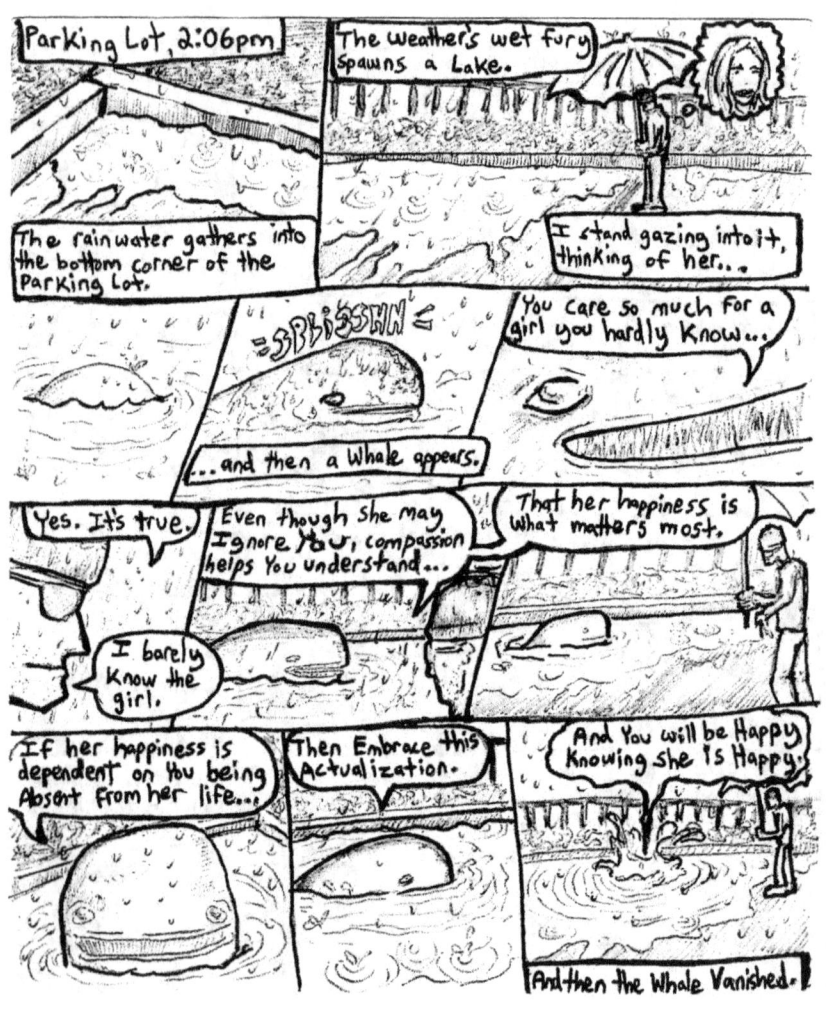

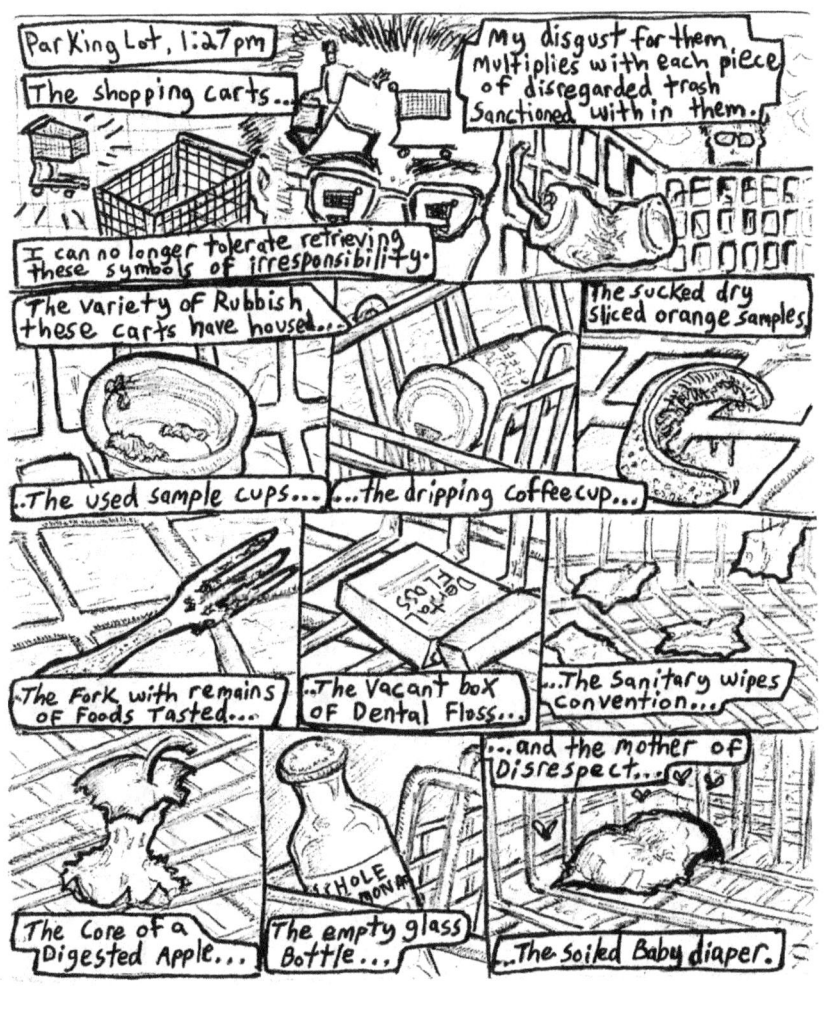

This is an image of me drawing on one of the infamous light pole ledge surfaces. This is where I spent most of my time creating the pages of Parking Lot Adventures. The stakeholders always thought I was writing some kind of parking ticket.

From a distance it looks pretty legit, like I'm really doing something important.

This was another great ledge to draw on. It was located in the far corner of the lot, nicely removed from most of the surrounding activities.

Sadly, it was also one of the most popular locations for shopping carts to accumulate.

A rare image of the parking lot guy in action taken by my
friend Tom Ryan during the summer time.

This photo was taken 2 weeks after I began my job in the
parking lot during my long hair recession depression phase.

This is the Last Place for Happiness. I built this claymation set as a place to allocate my fractured faith in humanity and regain my high spirits and natural cheeriness.

Animating clay became a terrific form of escapism, to be consumed by assorted fictional creatures and characters, the farthest thing from human beings that I could sculpt and then surround my self with. This is a photo of me trying to appear cool in front of the set.

Scenes from "Holiday Weekend" the extreme zombie claymation series I began producing after my deperture from the lot.

After a solid year and 2 months working in the parking lot I had produced enough claymation content to release my "Tales of Isolation" DVD! I immediately resigned from my position as the parking lot attendant, had thousands of DVD's manufactured, and then hit the road! Here is a photo of me at the Philadelphia Wizard World comic book convention behind my very own table promoting and selling my incredible life changing DVDs.

Photo Taken by F.Paul Galeone

This is my actor headshot as Mr.Oz. I look totally chilled out just leaning on the ladder. Now with my parking lot days behind me, I continue my voyage to Hollywood as Mr.Oz. Until then, I would like to sincerely thank you the reader for divulging into my exciting world of Parking Lot Adventures and please Stay Tuned!

Special Ever Lasting Thanks to the cast & crew of the Mr.Oz Show, Brendan Wall, Drew Panckeri, Tom Ryan, Philip Kessler, Curtis Lowery, The WDS, and my very amazing and fascinating family.

Check out my claymations and other wild videos by visiting these links!

www.talesofisolation.com
www.YouTube.com/talesofisolation
www.mrozshow.com
www.YouTube.com/mrozshow